Day at the Docks

Illustrated by The Artful Doodlers

Random House 🏠 New York
Thomas the Tank Engine & Friends™

CREATED BY BRITT ALLCROFT

Based on The Railway Series by The Reverend W Awdry. © 2010 Gullane (Thomas) LLC.
Thomas the Tank Engine & Friends and Thomas & Friends are trademarks of Gullane (Thomas) Limited.
HIT and the HIT Entertainment logo are trademarks of HIT Entertainment Limited.
All rights reserved. Published in the United States by Random House Children's Books, a division of Random House, Inc., 1745 Broadway, New York, NY 10019, and in Canada by Random House of Canada Limited, Toronto. Step into Reading, Random House, and the Random House colophon are registered trademarks of Random House, Inc.
www.stepintoreading.com   www.randomhouse.com/kids   www.thomasandfriends.com

Educators and librarians, for a variety of teaching tools, visit us at
www.randomhouse.com/teachers
ISBN: 978-0-375-85368-5   MANUFACTURED IN CHINA

HiT entertainment

Thomas tells Toby

he is going to see Rocky.

Toby wants to go, too.

They go to see Rocky at the Docks.

They are at the Docks.

But where is Rocky?

There is Rocky!

Rocky sits in the sun.

Rocky likes the sun.

Rocky sees Thomas and Toby.

He peeps hello to them.

They peep hello, too.

Thomas and Toby can pull.

There are mops to pull.

Do they want some mops?

They tell Rocky

they do not want mops.

There are dolls to pull, too.

Do they want some dolls?

They do not want

to pull dolls.

Look!

Rocky has shells to pull, too.

Thomas and Toby want

to pull all the shells!

Thomas and Toby take
the shells to the shed.